Starring CARMEN!

By
ANIKA DENISE

Illustrated by
LORENA ALVAREZ GÓMEZ

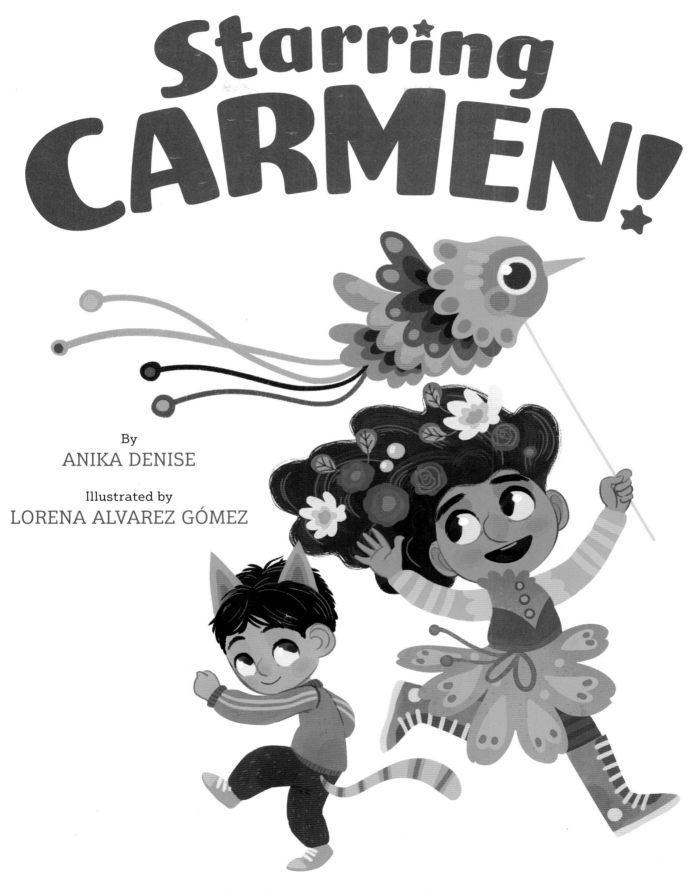

Abrams Books for Young Readers
New York

Carmen is a one-girl

SENSACIÓN!

She is an actress,
a singer, a dancer,
and a costume designer.

She does a new show every night.

"Kindly turn off your mobile devices," says Carmen.

The sets are elaborate. And the plot has a few surprising twists.

It's exhausting, but . . .
"That's showbiz!" says Carmen.
"*A dormir*, ninja *niña*," says Carmen's dad.

Before bed, Carmen practices her vocal exercises, because tomorrow's performance is a musical.

Dress rehearsals start early.
"Can I be in your show tonight?" asks Eduardo.
"Sure! I'm the queen. You can be a rock."
"How do I *be* that?" asks Eduardo.
"Don't move," says Carmen.

"Do I have any lines?"
asks Eduardo.

"Shh," says Carmen.
"Rocks can't talk."

It's **SHOWTIME!**
Carmen flickers the lights to let everyone
know the performance is about to start.

"What do I do?" whispers Eduardo.
"Wear this," says Carmen.
"But I thought I was a rock," says Eduardo.
"You make a better lamp."

There are seventeen
songs in Carmen's musical.
And twelve dance numbers.
And some karate.

When the curtain closes,
Carmen takes a bow—and exits stage left.

"Hello?"

Later, at dinner,
Carmen announces an **ENCORE!**

"You wear us out, *querida*,"
says Carmen's mom.
"*Sí, Carmenita*, we need a break from
show business," says Carmen's dad.

"But the show must go on," says Carmen. She pretends her toys are the audience, but it's not the same without the applause.

The following day, Carmen
doesn't feel like rehearsing.

She feels like sulking.

Carmen is a very
dramatic sulker.

"Why so grumpy, Grumperella?" asks Carmen's dad.
"Because I can't be a **STAR** without an **AUDIENCE!**"
"Well, I know someone who thinks you're a star,"
says Carmen's mom.

"It's my first fan mail," Carmen says softly.
"He loves you, *mija*, even when you make him
    wear a lampshade on his head," says Carmen's mother.

Carmen wants to tell Eduardo how much she likes his drawing.
"Eduaaaardo! Mi hermanito favoriiiiiito!" Carmen sings.

"There you are. What are you doing?" asks Carmen.

"Playing pirate ship," says Eduardo.

"Can I play, too?"

"Sure. I'm the captain. You can be my prisoner."

"How do I *be* that?" Carmen asks.

"Shh," says Eduardo. "Prisoners can't talk."

Captivity gives Carmen time to think.

"You know what?" Carmen says at last.

"I've always wanted to direct."

LITTLE LAMPSHADE PRODUCTIONS

— PRESENTS —

A ROCK OPERA

WRITTEN + DIRECTED BY
CARMEN!

STARRING EDUARDO

WITH COSTUMES BY CARMEN!

MUSIC BY DAD

MILK + COOKIES BY MOM

There are eleven songs
in Eduardo's Rock Opera.
And a puppet show.
And some robots.

But the **BEST** part,
if you ask Carmen . . .

. . . is the **SURPRISE** ending.

FOR BRANDON, MI HERMANITO FAVORITO.
—A.D.

TO ELENA, MY MOM.
—L.A.G.

The illustrations in this book were made with with paper, pencils, and Photoshop.

Cataloging-in-Publication Data has been applied for
and may be obtained from the Library of Congress.

ISBN: 978-1-4197-2321-6

Printed and bound in China
10 9 8 7 6 5 4 3 2 1

For bulk discount inquiries, contact specialsales@abramsbooks.com.

ABRAMS The Art of Books
115 West 18th Street, New York, NY 10011
abramsbooks.com